characters created by
lauren child

I really, REALLY need actual ice skates

PUFFIN

Charlie and Lola™

Text based on the script written by Bridget Hurst

produced by Tiger Aspect

Illustrations from the TV animation

PUFFIN BOOKS
Published by the Penguin Group: London, New York, Australia,
Canada, India, Ireland, New Zealand and South Africa
Penguin Books Ltd, Registered Offices: 80 Strand, London WC2R 0RL, England

puffinbooks.com

First published 2009
1 3 5 7 9 10 8 6 4 2
Text and illustrations copyright © Lauren Child/Tiger Aspect Productions Limited, 2009
The Charlie and Lola logo is a trademark of Lauren Child
All rights reserved
The moral right of the author/illustrator has been asserted
Made and printed in China
ISBN: 978-0-141-38474-0

I have this little sister Lola.
She is small and very funny.
Today Lola is really excited.
"Look, Charlie! We've got a letter."

Dear Charlie and Lola,
You remember we promised you some money so you could both buy scooters. Well, here it is. Scoot well.
All our love,
Granny and Grandpa.

"YES!"

says Lola.

And I say,
"I've wanted a
scooter for ages."

When we see Marv and Morten, I can't wait to tell them.

"We're getting **scooters** tomorrow!"

"Great!" says Marv.
"AND my mum is taking
us all to the new
ice-skating rink
after school today."

And Lola says,
"Ooh, ice skating!"

At school, Lola says,
"Lotta! Lotta! Are you
coming ice skating
with us today?"

And Lotta says,
"Yes, yes, yes!
I love ice skating."

Morten says,
"So do I!"

Lola says, "I'm going to do ice skating...

ice twisting...

"Look!" says Lotta.

"Oooh," says Lola. "Evie's got ice skates that are REAL. And I don't have ANY ice skates!"

"But I really do think I need
to have my OWN ice skates,
just like Evie...
with shiny silvery
bits on the bottom,
and ever-so-sparkly laces."

"Don't worry, Lola,"
says Evie.
"You can borrow
ice skates
when you
get to the
ice rink..."

At the **ice rink**, I say,
"Come on, Lola!"

And Lola says,
"It's w^obble-o^b-erley!"

"Look at me!" says Marv.

"I can do stopping!"
says Morten.

"Ooh, careful,"
says Lola.

"Yes, careful!"
says Lotta.

"Look at Evie!" says Lola.

"She can go backwardy," says Lotta.

"Yes," says Lola, "backwardy."

Marv says,
"I want to come again REALLY soon!"

"So do I!" says Lotta.

"So do I!" says Morten.

"You know, Charlie,
I really do think I
absolutely and
EXTREMELY
must have
my OWN
skates."

"But we're getting the
scooters tomorrow...
with Dad," I say.

And Lola says,
"I'm going to have real ice skates
instead of the scooter, Charlie –
because then I will be a
VERY good and very
twirlyish ice-skaterer...

"... I will be the best ice-skaterer

in the WHOLE of the school!"

When we get home, I say,
     "Maybe you should have
ice-skating lessons first,
          in case you don't really
want them after all..."

And Lola says,
     "But I DO really want them, Charlie!
I really, really, REALLY do!"

"But Lola, what about that **big,** red **kite** you really, really wanted?

And that toy **guitar** that you really, REALLY wanted, and never ever really, really played?

AND...

that special lighting-up **yo-yo** you really, really wanted?

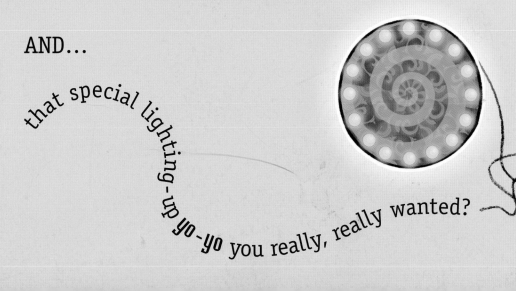

You'd better go and ask Dad."

"Dad said yes! Charlie! He said yes!"

"Are you sure, Lola?"

And Lola says,
"Absolutely, completely and EXTREMELY sure.
Dad said I must be very,
very good and promise not to change my
mind and that he doesn't want to find the
skates in the bottom of the cupboard."

The next day, we see
Marv and Morten.
I say,
"Like my new scooter?"

Marv says,
"Yep!"

And Morten says,
"Oops!"

Lola says,
    "Do you want to see my
really, really new ice skates?"

And Morten says,
    "They're good, Lola."

    And Lola says,
"I can't wait to do ice skating!"

At the ice rink,
    Lola says,
"Oh!"

And Lotta says,
    "Are your ice skates
good, Lola?"

Lola says,
    "Yes! It's just a little
bit tricky at the moment,
because, you see,
    they have never been
on the ice before..."

And I say,
"Come on,
hold my **hand**."

Then Lola falls over.
"I don't want
to have ice skates
any more, Charlie!"

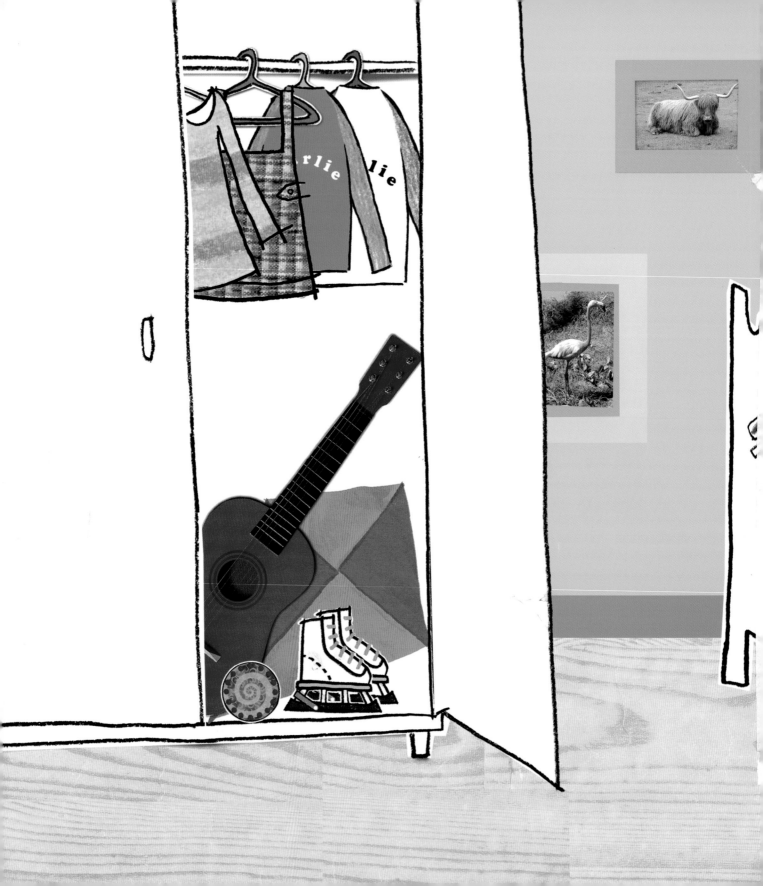

I say,
"You did really, REALLY want **ice skates**...
You just have to practise."

And Lola says,
"Maybe..."

The next time we go ice skating,
Lola sees Morten fall off his scooter.

"Oh!" says Morten.
"I think I don't like scootering very much."

And Lola says, "I don't think I am very
keen on ice skating, actually...

Do you think our dads would let us do SW∀PS?"

And Morten says,
        "They might!"

"I'm a good scooterer!"
        says Lola.

"I'm a really good ice-skaterer!"
says Morten.

Then Lola sees Evie...

Boing!

Boing!

and says,
"Oooh!
That looks fun..."